P9-ELS-651

KEEKER

and the Pony Camp Catastrophe

Milky Way is a registered trademark of Mars, Inc. Butterfinger
is a registered trademark of Nestlé. Milk Duds and Twizzlers are
registered trademarks of of The Hershey Company.

Series design by Kristine Brogno and Mary Beth Fiorentino.
Book design by Mariana Oldenburg.
Typeset in Weiss Medium.
The illustrations in this book were rendered in Adobe Illustrator.
Manufactured in China.

Library of Congress Cataloging-in-Publication Data
Higginson, Hadley.
Keeker and the pony camp catastrophe / by Hadley Higginson ;
illustrated by Lisa Perrett.
p. cm.
Summary: Ten-year-old Keeker is excited about going to
sleep-over pony camp, until she finds that one of her bunk
mates is her rival Tifni.
ISBN-13: 978-0-8118-5596-9 (library edition)
ISBN-10: 0-8118-5596-1 (library edition)
ISBN-13: 978-0-8118-5597-6 (pbk.)
ISBN-10: 0-8118-5597-X (pbk.)
[1. Camp—Fiction. 2. Horses—Fiction. 3. Animals—Infancy—
Fiction. 4. Friendship—Fiction.]
I. Perrett, Lisa, ill. II. Title.
PZ7.H53499Ked 2007
[E]—dc22
2006020958

Distributed in Canada by Raincoast Books
9050 Shaughnessy Street, Vancouver, British Columbia V6P 6E5

10 9 8 7 6 5 4 3 2 1

Chronicle Books LLC
680 Second Street, San Francisco, California 94107

www.chroniclekids.com

KEEKER

and the Pony Camp Catastrophe

by **HADLEY HIGGINSON** Illustrated by **LISA PERRETT**

chronicle books · san francisco

Chapter

This is Catherine Corey Keegan Dana, but everyone calls her Keeker.

Keeker is ten. She lives on a farm in Vermont with her parents, five dogs, three cats, a goat, two birds, and some tadpoles in a jar.

She has a best friend named Polly. And a sneaky pony named Plum.

All year Keeker looks forward to summer, because summers are SO fun. Keeker and Polly get together a couple of times a week to play dress-up, make forts, ride ponies, and go down to the lake to swim and eat ice cream. Summertime goes by so quickly, Keeker tries to cram in as much as possible.

Plum does NOT try to cram in as much as possible. Sometimes she plays with Goatie, but

usually she just likes to laze around under her apple tree, waiting for the fruit to fall.

One afternoon, before summer had even started, Keeker and Polly were up in Keeker's room, and Polly said something surprising.

"I'm going to France this summer with my parents."

"WHAT?" said Keeker. She couldn't believe it. What was there to do in FRANCE, anyway? What about the lake and pony riding?

But it was true. Polly was going away all summer, and her pony, Taffy, would be taking it easy. Keeker and Plum were going to be on their own.

After Polly went home, Keeker was very sad. She tried playing dress-up by herself, but it wasn't much fun waving a wand around alone.

Then she went outside to see what Plum was doing. Plum, of course, was dozing by the apple tree, doing exactly nothing.

"I'm bored," said Keeker, out loud. Plum opened one half of one eye and then closed it again so Keeker wouldn't know she was awake.

"I wish Keeker would stop waving that wand around," thought Plum. "What's she trying to do—turn me into a frog?"

That evening, right after dinner, Keeker's mom called Polly's mom.

"I'm a little worried about Keeker," whispered Mrs. Dana. "She's so sad that Polly won't be

# here this summer. She feels like there's nothing fun to look forward to."

"Well," said Polly's mom, "you should give Marge Snodder a call. Marge's daughter goes to sleepaway pony camp every summer and loves it. I think it's called Camp Kickapoo. And do you want to know the best thing? The ponies get so much exercise that they have no time to be naughty. It's great."

"Hmmmm," said Keeker's mom. "That sounds perfect for Keeker AND Plum!"

After she got off the phone, Keeker's mom hurried back into the kitchen.

"Cheer up, sweetie," said Mrs. Dana. "Polly's mom just gave me an idea. How about going to pony camp?"

"Wow," thought Keeker. "Camp. With Plum. Could be fun!"

Chapter 2

The next morning, Keeker went down to visit Plum, to see if she looked like she wanted to go to camp. Keeker looked deep into Plum's eyes. Plum peered at Keeker suspiciously.

"What's Keeker up to? She has that odd look again."

Plum had a sneaky feeling this summer was not going to be a lazy one!

And, of course, she was right. About a
month later, when summer was underway, Plum
was rolling around in her dirt patch when she
heard some VERY familiar sounds. *Rattle, rattle.
Clank. Thump.*

"Oh, no," thought Plum. "Not that thing
again! Where are we going now?"

It didn't seem fair. Goatie never had to go
anywhere!

Plum decided to hide. She found a patch of tall grass and lay down in it. It was lovely.

She couldn't see anything but green grass all around and bright blue sky overhead.

"It's like I'm invisible," Plum thought happily. She closed her eyes.

Munch, munch, munch. Plum heard chomping sounds and opened one eye. There was Goatie, chewing clover and staring at her.

"Go away!" Plum snorted. "Shoo! They'll know I'm here!"

But it was too late. Standing right behind
Goatie was Keeker's dad, holding a lead rope
and Plum's red halter. "Drat," thought Plum.

"Good try, Plum," said Keeker's dad. "But not
quite sneaky enough!"

It took four carrots, an apple, and two big handfuls of grain to convince Plum to get in the trailer.

But, finally, she did. And off they went.

When they arrived at Camp Kickapoo, the first stop was the barn so they could unload Plum and get her settled. Plum was in B Barn with the ponies. (Some of the older kids had horses, and they were in A Barn.)

Plum's stall was right in the middle of B Barn.
On her right was a very tiny, very old pony
named Zingo. On her left was a much younger
pony who looked familiar, although Plum
wasn't quite sure why.

"Hmmmm," thought Plum, "I could swear I
know that pony."

Once Plum was comfy (and all her camp
stuff was unpacked), Keeker and her parents

hopped back into the truck and headed up to the camp cabins.

Keeker leaned out the window as far as she could, so she could catch a sneak peek at Camp Kickapoo's sleeping cabins. And when she saw them, she couldn't believe it—it looked EXACTLY the way a camp ought to!

There was even a dog snoozing in the sun outside the office.

"I like it," Keeker said with a smile.

Chapter 3

A girl came bounding out of the camp office to greet them.

"Hello, Danas!" said the girl. "I've been expecting you. My name's Jenny. Welcome to Camp Kickapoo!"

Jenny grabbed Keeker's bags and led them around the corner to the very first cabin.

"This is Hedgehog House, where we like to

put our youngest campers," said Jenny, grinning
at Keeker.

Piled up outside Hedgehog House were
some very fancy bright blue suitcases. Something about them really, really reminded Keeker
of someone, but she couldn't quite think of who.

"Keeker, HI!" said Tifni, charging through the door. "Remember me?"

"Oh, yeah," thought Keeker. "That's who the suitcases reminded me of!"

Tifni seemed to have forgotten all about the fact that Keeker won the blue ribbon instead of her at last year's horse show. In fact, she seemed very glad to see Keeker. She grabbed Keeker by the elbow and dragged her into the cabin.

Inside the cabin was another girl, sitting on the bed and looking absolutely miserable.

Tifni looked at the girl and sighed. "That's Virginia," said Tifni. "She doesn't talk. Her pony is Zingo."

Keeker looked at Virginia. Tifni looked at Virginia. Virginia just stared straight ahead and didn't say a word.

That night Keeker and Tifni and Virginia
met the other campers and their counselors and
had a cookout. Tifni spent the whole evening
telling everyone how wild her pony Windsong

was and how she was the ONLY one who could control her. Keeker talked to a very tall girl about how fun it was to jump jumps.

Virginia still didn't say a thing.

After dinner everyone went back to their cabins. Since Keeker and Tifni and Virginia were the youngest campers, Jenny walked them back to Hedgehog House and made sure they all brushed their teeth.

"Good niiiiiiiiight, kiddos!" said Jenny, in a sing-songy voice, as she flicked off the lights. "When you hear the wake-up bell tomorrow morning, put on your riding clothes and come on down to the picnic tables for breakfast."

The door banged shut. It was very dark in the cabin. And very, very quiet. Keeker felt a big wave of homesickness swoosh over her.

"Tifni?" whispered Keeker.

"Yes?" whispered Tifni.

"Virginia?" whispered Keeker.

Silence.

Chapter

4

Fortunately for Keeker and Virginia, Tifni was an experienced camper—she knew EXACTLY how to cure homesickness. Tifni hopped off the bottom bunk and began rustling around in her suitcases.

She pulled out a pink knapsack, unzipped it, and dumped some stuff onto her bed. "Ta da!" said Tifni. She flicked on her flashlight, and there was the biggest pile of candy Keeker had ever seen.

Butterfingers. Twizzlers. Milky Ways and Milk Duds. The works!

"I love Milk Duds," said Virginia shyly.

"Hooray!" said Keeker. "You DO talk!"

After that everything was fine. The three of them stayed up VERY late, talking and eating candy. Tifni even fell asleep on the floor, lying in a big pile of Milky Way wrappers.

It seemed like they only got to sleep for a
minute before—*BONG! BONG! BONG!*—the
wake-up bell was clanging.

"Ooooof," said Keeker.

"Mnnnnnnn," said Virginia.

Tifni just groaned and started picking candy
wrappers out of her hair.

No one in Hedgehog House really felt like
going riding.

Plum didn't really feel like going riding, either. She did feel like having breakfast, though. Where was it?

"Here it is," said Keeker, grumpily, suddenly appearing at the stall door. She dumped two cups of sweet feed into Plum's bin and stomped off to get some brushes and her saddle.

"Hmmm, Keeker doesn't look so good," thought Plum. "Maybe today will be a short riding day."

Plum let her mind drift off to thoughts of blackberries and apples and her sunny field. But even in her daydream, Goatie was there to bug her.

Once the ponies were groomed and saddled, everyone headed over to the main ring to be divided into groups. The Hedgehog House riders—Keeker and Tifni and Virginia—were in the "elementary" group.

"What does that mean?" Keeker asked Virginia.

"It means we're the baby group," said Virginia with a sigh. "It means we probably won't get to jump very big jumps."

"Oh," said Keeker. She didn't like the sound of that at all.

For their very first lesson at Camp Kickapoo, Keeker and Tifni and Virginia worked on what they call gymnastics. At first Keeker thought that was very weird—she couldn't imagine Plum on a balancing beam! But as it turned out,

"gymnastics" just meant trotting over poles on the ground and jumping lots of little teeny-tiny jumps in a row.

"Bor-ring," thought Plum. "I could do this in my sleep!"

Off in the distance, Keeker could see the big girls on their big horses jumping BIG jumps—gates and water jumps and triple combinations. It looked fun.

That night, Tifni, Keeker, and Virginia ate up the last of the candy and talked about what they'd done that day.

"It was OK, I guess," said Keeker, "but I wish they'd let us jump big jumps!"

"I know," said Tifni. "My cousin was in the advanced group last summer, and she said there's a jump called the Table that's, like, five feet wide!"

"There's another one that's a drop jump, where you have to jump down big dirt STAIRS," said Virginia.

"Yeah," said Keeker. "I saw one that looked like a wagon, with hay on it and everything! But are we going to be just stuck trotting over poles the whole time we're here?"

"Probably," said Tifni. And they all went to bed grumpy.

Chapter 5

The next morning, the wake-up bell clanged extra early (or, at least, it seemed it did). Jenny came bouncing into the cabin like she'd been up for hours (and, actually, she had).

"Goooood morning, Hedgehog House!" said Jenny. "Rise and shine! Up and at 'em! Today you guys are going trail riding!"

"I can't believe this," thought Keeker. "That's what I do at home all the time. Why did I even bother coming to camp?"

But she and Tifni and Virginia got up and got dressed anyway and headed off to breakfast. Then they went down to the barn to tack up the ponies and meet up with Jenny and her horse, Dot.

"OK, guys, follow me!" said Jenny. "Stay in a line, OK?"

"What are we—six?" whispered Virginia.

They set off in a line, going VERY slowly. Even though it was a nice day, it was pretty dull—Plum and Zingo just kinda trudged along. Zingo appeared to be sleepwalking; his eyes were almost completely closed.

Plum wasn't asleep, but she was very day-dreamy and thinking about home. "Goatie has probably eaten all my apples," she thought. She imagined a little fence around her tree—one that she could reach over but that Goatie couldn't.

Windsong was the only pony that seemed antsy. She was walking WAY too close to Dot, and Jenny was talking so much she didn't even notice. Windsong started prancing in place.

Then, something startled her, and she scooted
forward and bumped Dot's tail.

As it turned out, Dot was very sensitive
about her tail. She squealed and kicked, and
Windsong whirled around and ran off. She
jumped the fence (with Tifni barely hanging
on) and started galloping down the road.

"Oh, no! Oh, no!" shrieked Jenny. "HELP!
RUNAWAY PONY!" She was completely
freaking out.

"C'mon Virginia," said Keeker. "We have to go after them!"

"Um, I don't think Zingo goes that fast!" said Virginia nervously.

"Sure he does," thought Plum. "Just look at him go!"

For the first time since they'd been at camp, Zingo's eyes were wide open.

Keeker and Plum and Virginia and Zingo jumped the fence and charged after Windsong, which made Jenny shriek even louder.

They galloped down the road, and when
Windsong zigzagged back into the field, Plum
and Zingo zigzagged right after her.

One after another, they jumped a ditch, galloped through a stream, and sailed over a hedge. Then, looming ahead, was the biggest jump any of them had ever seen.

The Table. All five-feet-wide of it.

Chapter

6

"Oh . . . my . . . gosh!" yelled Tifni. "Whoa, Windy, WHOA!" She sawed back and forth on the reins as hard as she could, but it didn't help at all. Windsong galloped right up to the jump, tucked her feet under her, and leaped a huge leap.

She jumped so big, in fact, that Tifni couldn't stay on. Tifni tumbled onto the ground in a very tidy ball and luckily didn't hurt herself.

Then Plum jumped. "Yikes!" thought Plum.
"Hold on!"

Amazingly, Keeker and Plum made it all the
way over. Keeker even managed to stay on—
even if she did end up around Plum's neck.

Last but not least came Zingo. He trotted up
to the Table, and then very delicately jumped . . .
on top of it.

"Nice view," thought Zingo. He cocked one
leg up underneath him and started chewing
on a piece of grass that had gotten stuck in
his bridle. Virginia flopped down onto Zingo's
back and sighed a huge sigh of relief.

Jenny caught up on her horse, looking very
flustered.

"You guys!" said Jenny, "that could have been
a TOTAL catastrophe! Is everyone all right?
Any injuries? Any broken bones?" Jenny started

poking and prodding Tifni to make sure she was all right.

"I'm FINE," said Tifni, trying to wave Jenny away. "Did you see that jump? Windsong jumped SO HIGH! And I ALMOST stayed on. Did you see how I ALMOST stayed on?"

"OK, I think we've all had enough excitement for one day," said Jenny. "Back to the barns. And this time, WALK!"

Everyone smiled a little at that.

Chapter
7

That night back at Hedgehog House, Tifni and Keeker and Virginia couldn't stop talking about what had happened.

"Wasn't that jump HUGE?" said Tifni.

"Yes!" said Keeker. "I was so scared. And what about Zingo? How funny was that? He was ON TOP of the Table!"

"I wish someone had taken a picture," sighed Virginia.

Just then, there was a knock on the door. Keeker went to open it, and there were two of the oldest, coolest girls at camp, with a big plate of chocolate chip cookies.

"We heard you all had a bit of a sweet tooth," said one of the girls, smiling. "And we heard

you had a pretty exciting day. So, enjoy. And congratulations on getting over the Table—I haven't even jumped that yet!"

As soon as they left, Tifni and Keeker and Virginia pounced on the plate.

"That was tho nith of them!" said Keeker, with her mouth full of cookie.

"I know!" said Virginia. "Plus, yum, chocolate chip cookies are the best. My mom makes them just like this."

"My mom isn't so good at cookies," admitted Tifni. "She usually burns them. But my dad and I eat them anyway. Although sometimes we give them to our dog Goober, when she's not looking."

The three of them munched and giggled till way too late. It was just about a perfect night.

Down in the barn, things were pretty peaceful. In fact, all three ponies were dozing cozily in their stalls. Zingo was remembering how it was when he was young and frisky, how HE had once been the wild one at Camp Kickapoo. Plum was still thinking about home and wondering if Goatie had found anyone new to bother.

And Windsong? Windsong was finally fast asleep, snoring daintily.

Everyone at camp—big girls and little girls, ponies and horses—was tucked into bed. Even the moon went behind a cloud to get a little rest. Only the stars stayed awake, streaking through the sky like runaway sparks.

Hadley Higginson grew up on a farm in Vermont where she had a sneaky pony of her own. She lives in Atlanta where she works as a writer for an advertising firm.

She no longer has a sneaky pony, but she does have a horse named Robbie and a bossy little dog.

To host an event with the
author of this book, please contact
publicity@chroniclebooks.com.

GALLOPING YOUR WAY IN SPRING 2008!

Introducing a new adventure in the Sneaky Pony series

KEEKER

and the Not-So-Sleepy Hollow

Summer is Keeker's favorite time for family road trips. When the whole family (even Plum and Goatie) drives to upstate New York to visit Keeker's aunt, uncle, and cousins in their big, new house, Keeker is sure it will be the best trip yet. (Plum, on the other hand, is not so sure!) Keeker is looking forward to splashing in the neighborhood pond and riding ponies in the country with her cousins. But what she doesn't know is that the nearby town of Sleepy Hollow holds a spooky secret, and Keeker will soon be swept up in the mystery. One thing's certain: This will be a memorable family vacation!

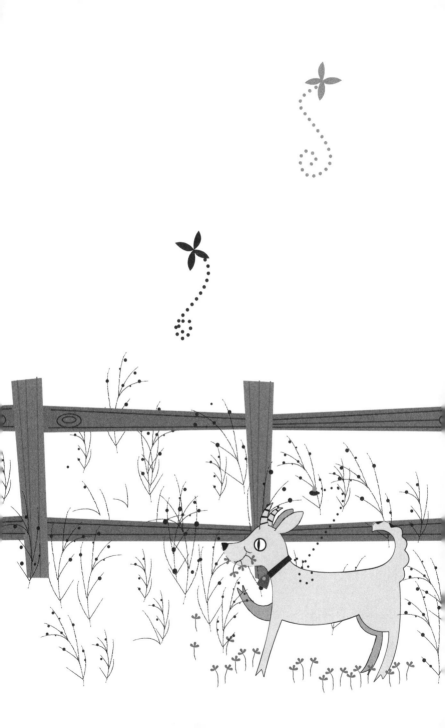